FEMDOM
College Punishments
Omnibus Edition

by Mistress Jade
(with Mark Maguire)

Published by
markmaguirebooks.co.uk

CONTENTS

**Adult consensual discipline stories
Involving corporal punishment, painful
caning, spanking and humiliation.**

Touch Your Toes, Brad!

by Mistress Jade (with Mark Maguire)

One of the best perks available to me in my position as Senior Mistress at St Boniface's Sixth Form College is the pleasure of punishing the young men who so frequently misbehave during their time here.

Today I am dealing with Brad Williams, who is going to suffer great indignity and pain as a result of handing in his essay late – for the second time.

Our sixth formers are all over 18, and as young adults they benefit from the hard corporal punishment I administer regularly to their bare bottoms. All of them, with no exceptions, on reaching the age of eighteen, willingly signed our standard consent form agreeing to whatever physical discipline we, as tutors, see fit to administer. Even though they are grown men, rudeness, laziness, smoking, truancy, bad manners and many other offences still need dealing with on a frequent basis – and this I very much enjoy doing – as a dominant, self-assured and sexy woman.

I punish each and every offence with painful corporal discipline which I always apply to bare bottoms – no exceptions. This aspect is often more of an ordeal for the young men to endure than the excruciating pain of one of my spankings or hard canings. They really dread the exposure of their most private parts to a woman – possibly more than the fiercely smarting buttocks they will have when they leave my study.

Many of the young men have girlfriends who will always, sooner or later, hear all the details of a punishment their handsome boyfriend has suffered. Can you imagine how embarrassing that is! This is why I love my job so much – the feeling of complete power I have over my young charges, combined with the pure enjoyment of watching the distress of a young man as he meekly presents his bare bottom for me to punish as I see fit. He and I both know that he will soon be bucking and writhing uncontrollably under the relentless burning sting of my expertly applied cane strokes. We both know also that his bottom will soon be displaying a fine collection of weals and red-raw ridges.

I love using my favourite, thin, whippy cane and I adore causing red raw stripes to appear across soft, firm male buttocks particularly if the buttocks I am punishing are beginning to be hairy.

I enjoy producing angry raised weals that will make sitting down more or less impossible for quite a while after the apologetic and regretful young man has left my study, clutching his throbbing cheeks in a desperate but futile attempt to rub out the maddening, burning sting.

I take great pride in the accuracy of my canings and can almost always produce an equal effect on both cheeks.

Today I am dealing with Brad Williams, a good-looking, strapping lad of 19 who made the mistake of handing his essay in several days late – for the second time this term.

A slim, tall young man about 6' 1" tall, with tousled light brown hair that falls over his eyes in a very appealing way, popular with the other lads and more particularly with the young women, many of whom find him irresistible, I know he will be dreading his visit to my study.

Here comes that meek, tentative knock on my door. I shall enjoy the next thirty minutes!

"Come in!"

"You wanted to see me Miss?"

"Shut the door, Brad. I can't say I WANT to see you, no. There are things I would rather be doing with my time. However, it is NECESSARY for me to see you, as I think you know. Remind us why you are here, please."

"Um ... I didn't hand my essay in on time, Miss."

"Precisely. And what did I warn you would happen if you failed to do this?"

"Um ... not sure Miss."

Brad is looking down at the carpet, shuffling slightly from foot to foot.

"Not sure, Brad? Not sure? Oh, young man, I think you are VERY sure, because I made myself VERY clear on this matter when I spoke about it to your class. Don't waste my time, Brad. Remind us both what I said would happen."

"You would cane me, Miss."

"Yes, Brad, and that is exactly what I am going to do. I am going to cane you. Just before we begin, and to make sure we both understand and know the drill in these matters, remind us please HOW I always administer a caning. Don't miss any details out, Brad, or I will DOUBLE the number of strokes you will receive."

"Um … er … you always cane bare … um … bottoms, Miss, and you always cane hard. You cane in doses of six strokes, Miss, and you …"

Here, Brad started to choke back tears which were forming in his eyes. My discipline was already having the desired effect on this recalcitrant young man.

One of my aims, in the discipline I gave, was always to make sure regret was complete by the time the young miscreant left me. This was surely already being achieved.

"Yes, Brad? I'm waiting. I think you know the other essential element of one of my canings, seeing as you've had several already."

"You always cane the lower half of my bottom, Miss."

"And why is that, Brad?"

"So that I will feel the effects when I try to sit down, Miss. So that I am reminded I've been caned whenever I sit down, Miss."

Brad said this bit twice, in two slightly different ways. I was pleased about this as it showed the psychological effect my impending punishment was having on this very nervous and regretful young man.

"Very well, Brad. I think we will begin. Remove your jacket, drop your trousers and pants, and then bend across my table, please. Stretch right across and grip the far side with your hands. Now, up on tip toe. Push your bottom right up and out, and part your legs as wide as they will go."

This was one of the parts I most enjoyed about the whole event. The presentation of the arse to be beaten had to be done to my entire satisfaction. I loved this bit.

Soon Brad' bare backside would be marked with the distinctive pattern of welts that my expert canings always produced. It would be a veritable riot of fiercely smarting horizontal lines all the way down from the crown of his beautiful arse to the extra-sensitive crease where his butt met his thighs.

The comparing of weals and red-raw ridges across their bottoms was a regular spectator sport in the dormitory. For now, I enjoyed his embarrassment as he got himself into the required completely submissive position.

I had instructed this young man to remove his own pants for me. When I was about to deal with an offender who I knew had only recently been punished, I always removed the pants myself. This was so that I could enjoy peeling down their tightly-fitting ultra-thin briefs, through which the raised stripes of the previous beating were always clearly visible. Slowly sliding a young man's underpants down over the rounded globes of his arse was always a great pleasure for me, especially if it was already displaying the painful results of a previous session of well-deserved corporal punishment.

I moved behind Brad and slightly to one side. I lifted the tail of his shirt and rolled it up onto his back, thus revealing the enticing sight of the bare buttocks about to be punished.

My expertise with the cane was legendary, having been achieved with an enormous amount of practice. I patted the soft buttocks, and ran my hands lightly over them, relishing the way they flinched and writhed under my touch and enjoying the feeling of the soft, downy hairs.

I adored Brad's bottom. It was a fine sight, and one of the most attractive of all those that I regularly punished. Beautifully proportioned, two big, smooth mounds of gorgeous masculine flesh were separated by a deep, inviting crack that sported quite a few dark brown hairs. I now had the perfect opportunity to cane it – hard – and give him a much-needed lesson. He would soon be another of our well-disciplined young men.

The challenge for me was to make him buck and writhe under the furious sting of the cane, while still keeping the strokes accurate, horizontal and evenly placed across the lower half of both beautifully-displayed buttocks. I always found the preliminaries exciting and deeply stimulating.

"Keep still, Brad. This will hurt!"

"Yes Miss."

Did I detect a slight raising further of that magnificent young male butt? Was Brad actually inviting the searing, scorching strokes he was about to receive? If this were the case, he would not be alone. Many of my young men came, sooner or later, to actually crave my fiercely-smarting, burning stripes, discovering for themselves the hidden benefits of painful corporal punishment.

Was Brad becoming an aficionado of the rod? Many of our badly behaved young men willingly admitted that the cane could be intensely arousing. This they would often admit to when anticipating a punishment session, or remembering one. They would feel much less this way, however, during the actual caning when the fire in their backsides would quickly become absolutely intolerable and inescapable. This will always produce very satisfying yelps and gasps that will sooner or later become uncontrolled howling – and then sobbing.

I remembered how nonchalant he had been when challenged about the lateness of his essay, and I therefore determined to punish him with fitting severity.

I began right across the crown of his arse. A swift, well-placed stroke that produced a clear welt right away, and caused the young man to hiss as he swayed from side to side in a desperate effort to cope with the pain.

THWHACK!

I have caned most of my sixth formers many times and it never ceases to amaze me how quickly they forget the absolutely excruciating pain a caning always produces. The first stroke always seems to take them by surprise – just how much it hurts. Soon he would have a raging fire in his backside that would burn and smoulder for many hours to come!

"Six strokes," I announced. Then added with a slight chuckle "... to begin with."

I really enjoy my role as Senior Mistress!

I gradually caned the whole lower surface of his roasting, bouncing behind. This would be an unforgettable lesson for him. I brought the second stroke in, a little harder, and a little below the first.

THWHACK!

Brad yelled and twisted as the pain penetrated deep into his outstretched bare buttocks and the beautiful scarlet ridges rose across his trembling arse. He shook his backside and bellowed with the agony my cane so effortlessly produced.

Even the most stoic of our young men will always give way eventually to unrestrained howling, spluttering and gasping while being caned as vigorously as I always did. Brad was reacting in this way already – and I had only just begun. I found that fact immensely exciting, and very rewarding.

THWHACK!

Stroke number three found its target as I whipped it in, right across the place where Brad would be wanting to sit down.

"AAAAAAAAAAAARGH! Oh please Miss! No Miss! I can't Miss! I can't stand it Miss!"

The handsome young man's robust cheeks bounced and flinched beautifully as they throbbed with each stroke.

I paused and swished the superb cane through the air.

"Oh but you CAN, Brad. You CAN take it, and you CAN stand it. It hurts like the very devil, doesn't it, young man? But it's good for you Brad. It teaches you to behave, doesn't it, Brad? It teaches you to hand your essays in on time, doesn't it Brad?"

"Yes Miss."

"What does it do, Brad?"

"It hurts like the very devil, Miss."

"Exactly! And that's the whole idea. That's what makes the cane such an excellent punishment. And what is this particular caning teaching you, Brad?"

"To hand my essays in on time Miss."

"Precisely. And now we will continue. We had reached stroke number three of your first six, I believe."

I said this brightly and cheerily, but it brought no response from the submissive young man who was sticking his naked, unprotected bottom out for me. He raised it a little more, offering more of that most sensitive area in his crease, opening his crack a little wider as he did so, giving me the first tantalising glimpse of his arse hole. I knew that his bottom was already on fire, but I could stoke up that heat a great deal more before I had finished. His arse would be literally sizzling with the heat when he left my study. I would make sure of that.

THWHACK!

Stroke number four was a beauty. It whipped right across the soft, lower areas of both of his manly cheeks, producing a bright red line of pain equally on each bare buttock.

Brad yelled and twisted his agonised bum. His shaking backside wobbled even more attractively as I waited patiently for it to subside again in complete submission. This it quickly did, before being poked UP again in open invitation for the next scorching, burning stroke of fire.

Oh, how I was enjoying myself, indulging in the art of traditional corporal punishment. Deeply stimulating was the effect it always had on me, and the best of our young men had grown to acknowledge this effect too – mixed, of course, with the excruciating pain and complete humiliation.

I tapped the cane very lightly across the place I decided to cane next. I rubbed it back and forth across the very lowest part of his outstretched bare butt, just a little lower than the previous stroke which had produced such an excellent response.

"Please Miss! Not there again Miss. Anywhere but there, please Miss!"

Brad pleaded with me to punish some other part of his bottom. A part he hoped wouldn't be quite so sensitive. However, I knew what I was doing. He already had four hot scarlet ridges etched horizontally across each of his manly cheeks. I knew they would be throbbing nicely by now.

Many years of practice had taught me that the most tender area of a young man's bottom – and therefore the area that would benefit the most from punishment – was the part where his buttocks met the tops of his legs. Known as the sit spot, cane strokes applied here produce at least double the effect of strokes applied higher up. I wasn't going to let Brad dictate where my strokes were going to land!

I made no reply to his pleadings and merely delivered the last two strokes of the first six QUICKLY and swiftly right into the crease of his underbottom. This produced the effect I was wanting to achieve.

THWHACK! THWHACK!

"AAAAAAAAAAAAAAAAAAAAAAAAARGH! OW! OUCH! AAH! OW! OH Miss!"

Brad' beaten bottom was now bouncing up and down, clenching and unclenching, while its owner wept and sobbed into the far side of my table. Brad still clung on to the edge of the table, still stuck his bottom UP, and still remained in this completely submissive and totally humiliating position.

His bum was a sight to be seen. Decorated with beautifully throbbing stripes, his slightly hairy crack opened and closed as his butt vibrated and jerked in agony. He wouldn't sit or sleep comfortably for several days, I felt sure. Both of us knew that, at this point. I hoped that Brad would remember his punishment for many days to come, and that his thoroughly sore bottom would throb continuously with that absolutely maddening sting through several days and nights. Hopefully, too, his bottom would remind him of his bad behaviour every time he tried to ease it onto a chair or bench. And both of us knew there was more on the way!

"Up you get, Brad!" I said, not unkindly. "There's more to come, young man, as I'm sure you realise. Another six strokes will complete your lesson for today."

"Yes Miss."

"And then you can report to me again at the same time tomorrow for a spanking. That will give you the opportunity to think once again about your mistake in handing in your essay late, and it will give me the opportunity to view your stripes before I spank you. I like to make sure my canings go home, so to speak, and by tomorrow, your stripes should have blossomed fully. If I don't feel they are showing clearly enough across both of your cheeks, I can always cane you again to reinforce the lesson."

"Oh that won't be necessary, Miss, I can assure you," Brad interjected. "I can tell already they're going to still be raised and throbbing this time tomorrow."

"Well I certainly hope so," I said. "And now into the corner please for half an hour's thinking time before you go back over the table for your other six strokes today. I hope you are finding your punishment beneficial."

"Yes Miss. Thank you Miss. Definitely Miss. Thank you VERY much for disciplining me Miss."

And as Brad walked over to the corner of my study, his thick young cock started to rise. By the time the young man arrived in the corner and placed his hands on his head, his cock was sticking proudly up in the air and was clearly throbbing as much as its young owner's arse. Oh how beneficial my discipline always proved to be!

In half an hour's time, I would make sure the next six strokes would be even more challenging for him. I would cane those robust and bouncy cheeks again, even more determinedly than before. I would apply those six further strokes with even more vigorous relish and then I would send him away to the jibes and laughter of his student colleagues as they watched him get ready for bed. His underpants would take a while to remove as he would have to peel them down very gingerly over his smarting, throbbing cheeks. He would be sleeping face down tonight.

Word would soon get round that he was to report to me AGAIN at the same time tomorrow and, of course, a hand spanking was so particularly embarrassing for a young man to have to undergo, over the knees of a mature, sexy woman. I would certainly make sure that his regret was complete! Brad was a delight to beat, and his response seemed to improve every time he reported to me. He was a popular young man, and part of his popularity was due to the way he let everyone know how well he appreciated my artistry with the cane.

Tomorrow his well-proportioned manly cheeks would be bouncing rhythmically over my knees as they wobbled and flinched in time with the urgent smacks of the flat of my hand. I couldn't wait. Femdom discipline always gets results!

The next story in this series is entitled "This will really HURT, Gary!" in which I describe in detail how I deal with a rather arrogant young man who needs bringing down a peg or two after he has been rude to one of my members of staff. He will certainly think twice before being rude again after I have finished with him. Read all about it!

This Will Really HURT, Gary!

by Mistress Jade (with Mark Maguire)

One of the best perks available to me in my position as Senior Mistress at St Boniface's Sixth Form College is the pleasure of punishing the young men who so frequently misbehave during their time here.

Today I am dealing with Gary Thomson, a handsome young man with rugged good looks, a swarthy complexion and come-here deep brown eyes who is going to be punished for rudeness. He will shortly discover just how much my favourite cane burns and stings as it penetrates deep into his obediently presented manly buttocks.

This is a detailed account of the punishments I gave him. He was foolish enough to argue with me about the bare bottom caning I decided he should have, and so had to report back a second time for a particularly painful encounter with the hard polished wooden back of my favourite hairbrush.

Our sixth formers are all over 18, and as young adults they benefit from the hard corporal punishments I administer regularly to their bare arses. All of them, with no exceptions, on reaching the age of eighteen, willingly signed our standard consent form agreeing to whatever physical discipline we, as tutors, see fit to administer. Even though they are grown men, rudeness, laziness, smoking, truancy, bad manners and many other offences still need dealing with on a frequent basis – and this I very much enjoy doing, as a mature, dominant and sexy woman.

I punish each and every offence with painful corporal discipline which I always apply to bare bottoms – no exceptions. This aspect is often more of an ordeal for the young men to endure than the excruciating pain of one of my spankings or hard canings.

Many of the young men have girlfriends who will always, sooner or later, hear all the details of a punishment their handsome boyfriend has suffered. Can you imagine how embarrassing that is! This is why I love my job so much – the feeling of complete power I have over my young charges, combined with the pure enjoyment of watching the distress of a young man as he meekly presents his bare bottom for an older woman to punish as I see fit.

I love using my favourite, thin, whippy cane and I adore causing red raw stripes to appear across their soft, firm male buttocks particularly if the buttocks I am punishing are beginning to be hairy. I enjoy producing angry raised weals that will make sitting down more or less impossible for quite a while after the apologetic and regretful young man has left my study, clutching his throbbing cheeks in a desperate but futile attempt to rub out the maddening, burning sting.

I take great pride in the accuracy of my canings and can almost always produce an equal effect on both cheeks. My hand spankings are never a soft option either. I persist with a spanking until I am sure I have got through to the recalcitrant young man over my knee. This only happens when he cries. It can take a long time for this to be achieved, but I always keep going until I do. "Spanked to tears" is my favourite motto and all the sixth formers in my charge know this.

Today I am dealing with Gary Thomson, a young man who is too fond of his own voice. He will speak without thinking, and will often interrupt my members of staff – quite rudely on occasions. I have made it clear to him that rudeness will always be dealt with severely, and even though he's been over my knee struggling, writhing and bawling his eyes out more times than I can remember, he's due here again today to be punished for his latest incident of rudeness when he interrupted one of my colleagues yesterday, going so far as to question the particular tutor's knowledge of his subject.

He will know that his time with me will be extremely painful, and will be acutely aware that he will be leaving with a well-beaten and throbbing arse.

Here comes that tentative knock on my door.

"Enter."

Gary appears, looking apprehensive – as well he might!

"Ah, Gary. Right on time, I'm pleased to see. Just as well, Gary as you're in enough trouble as it is, and you wouldn't have appreciated the extra punishment I always give for lack of punctuality."

"No Miss."

The handsome young man's tight black trousers fitted perfectly around his attractive rump, accentuating the two beautiful buttocks and the deep cleft in between. He would remove his trousers himself, I decided, but I would keep the pleasure of pulling down his pants for myself.

"Come and stand here, Gary. Stand up straight lad, hands by your sides and don't slouch or fidget."

"Yes Miss."

"We will discuss why you are here in a moment, young man, but first of all, you will be kind enough to bring me a cane. You know where they are kept. Go over to the pot in the corner and select one that you think will be appropriate for punishing a young man who has too much to say, and who needs to learn manners."

I always enjoyed seeing a miscreant choosing his own instrument of torture. All my canes hurt like absolute blazes. They are all designed for that purpose and carry it out magnificently. However, it gives me extra pleasure and not a little amusement to see a young man fiddling with them and trying to decide which one will inflict the least amount of pain. In my skilled and experienced hands, all my canes are truly lethal, so it matters not one jot which one Gary will select!

My sixth formers' bottoms are all different, but of course in some ways the same. Whether hairy or smooth, whether small, medium sized or large, they will all clench, writhe and wobble when suffering under the relentless sting of my expertly applied scorching strokes.

Gary already knows that. He chooses a strong, sturdy rattan, about 30" in length with a traditional crooked handle. It's wickedly whippy and will undoubtedly produce absolutely breath-taking agony from the very first accurate, punitive swipe.

"Bring it here, Gary. Put the cane on the table where you can see it while you tell me why you are going to feel it across your bare bottom this afternoon."

Blushing bright red, the young man gingerly placed the cane on my desk, no doubt marvelling at how something so light and slender could be capable of causing such extreme pain and distress.

"I'm waiting, Gary."

"I'm afraid I interrupted Mrs Wilson, Miss."

"So I understand. And what, pray, did you say?"

"She was going on and on about the second world war and I just lost interest, I suppose. I told her she was being too slow in her descriptions of the battles and that they were rather repetitive anyway."

"How dare you, Gary!" I bellowed. "How dare you question one of my members of staff."

"But it was all just too boring, Miss."

"Are you pushing your luck, Gary? Do you seriously imagine I care whether or not you found Mrs Wilson's lesson boring?"

"No Miss."

"Take down your trousers, Gary and step right out of them. We'll start dealing with the matter of your rudeness right now. Fold them neatly and place them on that chair. Now go over to the corner and stand facing the wall with your hands on your head. Let's have that nose of yours touching the wall, Gary. Stay quite still and we'll see if you find half an hour's corner time BORING."

I would really enjoy the next thirty minutes. With his hands on his head, his shirt rode up, revealing the two sturdy masculine buttocks I would soon be beating. They were still encased in the thin white cotton briefs that were regulation wear for all sixth formers, but I would be pulling those down before caning those beautiful masculine mounds of soft flesh.

The lowest part of both cheeks was where I liked to concentrate my canings. This would be the part he would attempt to sit down on after his punishment – and this would be extremely painful to do once I had finished with him! This is the softest and most tender area of any young man's bum, and this particular young man would soon be sporting some deep red tram-lines across the lower half of both his manly cheeks. As I watched him try to stand completely still, I wondered whether this particular bottom was a hairy one. Many of my young men had hairy bums. Even if the cheeks were not particularly hairy, almost all of them had developed quite hairy cracks which I always enjoyed seeing displayed for me. I would soon be applying the thin pliant cane to his unprotected buttocks, causing acute pain from the very first stroke. Gary knew this while he was standing there. And he also knew that I knew! Thereby, confirming the wonderful psychological effects that corporal punishment always achieves, in addition to the harsh physical pain.

Gary would soon be offering up his bare arse for a really good beating. I couldn't wait – but I would not begin until the full thirty minutes were up.

Eventually I said brightly

"Come here, Gary. The time has come to beat you."

Quivering slightly with both fear and embarrassment, the young man approached me, looking down at the carpet all the time.

"Turn around."

The moment had arrived. With real relish, I grasped the waistband of his briefs and tugged them all the way down to his ankles. I was rewarded with the view of two perfectly formed hairy buttocks just crying out to be beaten.

"Step out of your pants, Gary. Pick them up and put them on the chair with your trousers. Now come over here and bend over. Bend right down and touch your toes – or as near as you can get to them!"

This was an athletic young man. His fingertips reached right down to his toes with very little effort. The effort, however, would be need in

STAYING down when my cane really began to sting!

"Legs apart, Gary. As far apart as they will go. I remind you to stay in that position no matter how much my caning hurts – and it will hurt a lot as I think you already know from previous visits to me."

I always insisted on a young man's legs being spread apart, as this spread his bum-cheeks open too. Gary had a delightfully hairy crack, and with his cheeks apart, I had an excellent view of his arsehole.

"Yes Miss." This reply was given quietly, speaking down towards the carpet.

"My canings are always given in sixes, and we shall see how many sixes you need this afternoon to teach you to be polite when speaking to your tutors. If your fingers leave your toes, I shall start that particular six again from the beginning. Is there anything you don't understand?"

"No Miss."

"Very good. Then we shall begin."

THWHACK!

Without warning, I brought the excellent cane in swiftly, right across the crown of his upstretched arse. It was a beautiful stroke that would act as a marker for what was to follow. I would now cane gradually lower and lower until I was punishing the soft crease of his underbottom – where his bum met the tops of his legs.

THWHACK!

The second, I felt sure, was another beauty, and I made sure it was applied a little harder as well.

"Aaaaaagh!"

"Did you have something to say, Gary? Did you have a comment to make?"

"No Miss. I couldn't help myself, Miss. It just HURT so much. The sting was absolutely intolerable and all-consuming."

"Very well put, Gary. You express yourself very well."

Before he could even begin to compose himself again that cruel Mistress 'cane whipped across his sore cheeks once more. I really was an expert at my craft!

THWHACK!

"AAAAAAAAAAAAARGH! OW! Oh Miss!"

"Cry out as much as you like Gary. Feel free to express yourself vocally – but don't let your fingers leave your toes or all of this will have been in vain and we shall start again from the very beginning."

"Oh Miss. Please Miss."

"Yes Gary?"

"Nothing Miss. Sorry Miss."

"Pleased to hear it Gary. Stick that bottom of yours right up, won't you!"

"Yes Miss."

THWHACK!

The fourth, even harder stroke landed. I was caning faster now, giving little time to recover from one stroke before the onslaught of the next. Gary yelled again in absolute panic as the fire in his blazing, beautifully striped arse increased even more.

Then everything changed. Now I was gently rubbing the cane on the young man's throbbing buttocks. It was gentle in the extreme, almost teasing as I lightly tapped and patted that terrible cane all over both of Gary's muscular mounds. As his legs were wide apart, I could see his balls hanging – and I could see his cock starting to grow. Its length increased and it became harder and harder, straining for relief as I continued gently tapping. As the cane lightly travelled across the surfaces of his naked cheeks it found the ridges it had so far created. I decided there were two more ridges for it to make before it had finished its job of punishing this handsome young man for today. I was famous for my "six of the best" canings. I never gave less than six strokes, though sometimes many more. I knew Gary would be hoping and praying that today would just be a six. For myself, I really didn't know if he would be able to take more.

The rubbing and patting stopped. Now I was swishing the cane menacingly through the air behind the submissive young man bent over and lewdly displaying his bum for my pleasure. His cock twitched and throbbed, but I didn't want him to know that I could see what it was doing.

Gary was pushing his bare bum up and out, involuntarily presenting it in the perfect position to be caned. Then he parted his legs even more.

"That's it, Gary. Part those legs as wide as they will

go. I'm going to punish the insides of your cheeks as well."

His cheeks parted more, spreading his bare buttocks wide open and offering his most sensitive and private parts of all to be punished. It would not be the first time that he had discovered that it's the soft areas on the inner cheeks that feel the pain the most.

"You can get that bottom higher than that Gary, I'm sure," I said, only adding to his complete humiliation.

Gary tried to comply and then, without warning, I began again, this time with a real vengeance.

THWHACK!

I whipped the springy cane smartly across both of his proffered cheeks. He cried out and desperately remained stretched down to his toes. His legs started to shake a little but he made sure he stayed in position.

"Keep that bottom UP Gary and keep your buttocks relaxed. Don't clench your cheeks."

My instructions were calm and very clear and he obeyed completely.

THWHACK! The sixth stroke landed just a little below his bottom, right across the tops of his thighs, hugely increasing the agony. He yelled and clung on for dear life, obediently sticking his bum right up as far as he could. His legs were spread wide and his arse was wide open also.

"AAAAAAAAAAAAAAAAAAAARGH! Ow! Oh Miss!"

Then he said more …

"Oh thank you Miss! Thank you for caning me Miss!"

"That was six of the best Gary."

"Six of the very best Miss!"

"And have you learned your lesson Gary? Are those beautiful stripes of yours going to remind you to speak politely to your tutors?"

I swished the cane through the air as I spoke. Gary remained in position, fingers on toes, arse in the air, throbbing and twitching slightly, legs shaking uncontrollably.

"Not sure Miss."

This was the reply I was hoping for. This young man really appreciated my efforts with the cane every time he visited me, and his swollen stiff cock was testimony to this. It stuck proudly up, defiantly saying to me "please cane my bottom some more Miss – and even harder this time please."

"Right Gary. I think we understand each other very well."

"We certainly do Miss."

"You're an addict, Gary."

"Yes Miss."

"Just two more strokes today, Gary."

And then a change stated to come over him. He pushed his bum up higher, he spread his legs as wide open as they could possibly go and arched his back, presenting his bare buttocks for the next strokes. I couldn't understand why, but I could see he was just begging me to cane him again. He wanted that burning hot fiery sting. I knew he craved it and he stuck his arse up in the air just waiting to feel that indescribable molten heat. I made sure it wasn't long coming.

THWHACK!

My cruel cane exploded once again across the lowest part of his writhing arse. I punished the meatiest part of his exposed posterior with the hardest stroke of the afternoon so far. He yelled out loud but stuck his blazing bum up still further. Before he had time to compose himself again, I brought in the final viciously stinging cut right across the tops of his legs. Everyone would be able to see what he had suffered when his bottom went on show in the showers, and my expertise as Senior Mistress with the cruel rod would be acknowledged once again.

"Stand up Gary."

As he stood, an agonised look was written across his handsome young face. His hands flew to his tormented sit-upon in a desperate but futile attempt to rub out the maddening pain.

"Put your clothes on Gary."

"Yes Miss."

"And I'm sure you don't need reminding that all my punishment appointments come in twos."

"Yes Miss. I do remember that. I remember very clearly Miss, from last time Miss."

His cock twitched even more vigorously as he said this.

"Good. Then report to me again at the same time tomorrow and we will continue where we left off today. You will regret being rude to your tutor, Gary. We will make sure of that tomorrow."

"Yes Miss. Thank you very much Miss. Thank you for disciplining me Miss. See you tomorrow Miss."

He grinned warmly and held out his hand to shake mine. As we clasped hands he added enthusiastically

"Wow that cane hurts!"

"I know, Gary," I confirmed. "That's the whole idea!"

The next story in this series is entitled "Bend Over, Russell!" in which I describe in detail how I deal with a cocky young man who needs a painful reminder to behave after he has been caught writing lewd graffiti. Russell will certainly think twice before scribbling on toilet walls again after I have finished with him. Read all about it!

Bend Over, Russell!

by Mistress Jade (with Mark Maguire)

One of the best perks available to me in my position as Senior Mistress at St Boniface Sixth Form College is the pleasure of punishing the young men who so frequently misbehave during their time here.

Today I am dealing with Russell Taylor, a strapping lad who is going to discover the painful consequence of scrawling lewd graffiti on one of the walls in the men's toilets.

Our sixth formers are all over 18, and as young adults they benefit from the hard corporal punishments I administer regularly to their bare bottoms. All of them, with no exceptions, on reaching the age of eighteen, willingly signed our standard consent form agreeing to whatever physical discipline we, as tutors, see fit to administer. Even though they are grown men, rudeness, laziness, smoking, truancy, bad manners and many other offences still need dealing with on a frequent basis – and this I very much enjoy doing as a dominant, mature, sexy woman who's very much in charge.

I deal with each and every offence with painful corporal punishment which I always apply to bare bottoms – no exceptions. This aspect is often more of an ordeal for the young men to endure than the excruciating pain of one of my spankings or hard canings.

Many of the young men have girlfriends who will always, sooner or later, hear all the details of a punishment their handsome boyfriend has suffered. Can you imagine how embarrassing that is! This is why I love my job so much – the feeling of complete power I have over my young charges, combined with the pure enjoyment of watching the distress of a young man as he meekly presents his bare bottom for an older woman to punish as I see fit.

I love using my favourite, thin, whippy cane and I adore causing red raw stripes to appear across their soft, firm male buttocks particularly if the buttocks I am punishing are beginning to be hairy. I enjoy producing angry raised weals that will make sitting down more or less impossible for quite a while after the apologetic and regretful young man has left my study, clutching his throbbing cheeks in a desperate but futile attempt to rub out the maddening, burning sting.

I take great pride in the accuracy of my canings and can almost always produce an equal effect on both cheeks. My hand spankings are never a soft option either. I persist with a spanking until I am sure I have got through to the recalcitrant young man over my knee. This only happens when he cries. It can take a long time for this to be achieved, but I always keep going until I do. "Spanked to tears" is my favourite motto and all the sixth formers in my charge know this.

Here then is my detailed account of how I dealt with Russell Taylor, our toilet wall graffiti "artist".

There's a quiet, tentative knock at my door. It's exactly two o'clock. This was one of the parts I most enjoyed about the whole event. I would keep the young man waiting – several minutes sometimes – while I knew his heart would be beating rapidly, and beads of sweat would be forming on his handsome forehead. When I was quite ready, and not before, I walked over to the door and opened it.

"Ah, Russell. What a pleasant surprise. Come in, won't you?"

We both walked into the room, one of us confident and assured, the other anxious and submissive.

"Stand there Russell, in front of my table. Begin, please, by reminding us both what you see waiting in readiness ON my table."

Russell's reply was so quiet, it was barely audible.

"Your cane, Miss."

"And what is it waiting in readiness FOR?"

"To punish me, Miss."

"Exactly, Russell. And which PART of you do you suppose it is going to punish?"

There was a long pause, during which the young man started to visibly tremble. Then he said

"My bum, Miss."

"Right again, Russell. Your BARE bottom, to be precise."

Even though this particular young man had been in this very situation before, he blushed bright red at this remark of mine."

"We have an art class in this college, Russell, run by Miss Fairhurst who is an excellent tutor and a very talented artist herself. She, like me, absolutely LOATHES graffiti. Obviously, I have told her I intend to cane you this afternoon, and what do you think she said when I told her?"

"Not sure, Miss."

"She recommended I cane you HARD, Russell, and that is exactly what I intend to do."

"Yes Miss."

"I don't know whether you call it art, young man, but WE certainly don't. The particular example which you so kindly treated us to, was scrawled in felt-tip pen on one of the cubicle walls in the men's toilets, I believe."

"Yes Miss."

"Would you be so kind as to remind us both what this piece of 'art' was meant to depict?"

"Um ... I'm not sure Miss."

"Then you'd better be sure very quickly, Russell. If you keep me waiting for any of the answers to what are the simplest of questions, you will suffer additional consequences as well as what I have already planned for you this afternoon."

"It was a drawing of a cock, Miss."

"A penis, Russell, is the term you will always use when talking to me, as an older woman. And what was this penis doing in this particular masterpiece of yours, pray?"

"It was sticking up, Miss. Rock hard, Miss … " (here Russell forgot himself and started to giggle) " and was dripping a bit of pre-cum Miss."

"Your language is as lewd as your drawings, Russell. And because you seem to be finding this whole thing amusing, I shall ensure that you do not leave my study with a smile on your face. You won't be smirking when I've finished with your bottom, I can assure you, and you won't be wanting to sit down either. Your bum is going to be burning, Russell. My excellent cane is going to produce some lovely read weals on your bare buttocks that will smart and sting like the very devil."

"No Miss. Yes Miss. Um … I mean no Miss. I mean … yes PLEASE Miss!"

Did I detect a slight grin still? Was he starting to play games with me? Was he actually INVITING more of my painful discipline? He wouldn't be the first young man to find my corporal punishment a turn-on, if that were the case. We would see, as the punishment progressed.

"Right, Russell. We'll waste no more time. I can see there is nothing to be gained by further discussion so we will start dealing with your disgusting offence right now. Drop your trousers and pants, and step out of them. Place them on the chair over there and then come over here."

Russell complied immediately, without hesitation. He wore attractive, skin-tight briefs which were revealed as his trousers were removed. They were thin, nylon, and very clinging. They were also to come down, as per my instructions.

As they were removed, Russell's thick uncut cock sprang into life. It started to rise as the young man walked towards me, and by the time he reached the edge of my table, it was getting pretty hard and pointing defiantly upwards.

I enjoyed this sight no end, but made no comment.

The presentation of the arse to be beaten had to be done to my entire satisfaction. With this in mind, I moved behind Russell and slightly to one side. I lifted the tail of his shirt and rolled it up onto his back, thus revealing the enticing sight of the bare buttocks about to be punished.

"Bend right across the table, Russell. Grip the far side and go up on tiptoe."

My expertise with the cane was legendary, having been achieved with an enormous amount of practice. I patted the soft buttocks, and ran my hands lightly over them, relishing the way they flinched and writhed under my touch and enjoying the feeling of the soft, downy hairs. Soon they would be bucking and writhing uncontrollably as I stoked up a raging fire across his arse. Russell undoubtedly pushed his bum up a bit more as I did this. Was he actually ASKING to be caned by an older, dominant woman?

I adored Russell's bottom. It was a fine sight, and one of the most attractive of all those that I regularly punished. Beautifully proportioned, two big, smooth mounds of gorgeous masculine flesh were separated by a deep, inviting crack that sported quite a few dark brown hairs. I now had the perfect opportunity to cane it – hard – and give him a much-needed and well-deserved lesson.

"Keep your bottom still, Russell. This will hurt!"

"Yes Miss. Yes please, Miss."

The young man could still afford to be just a little cheeky at that point. Once the first stroke had registered, however, he would quickly change his tune. All my young men FORGOT just how intolerably my canings burned and stung, no matter how many times it had happened to them.

THWHACK!

"AAAAAAAAAAAAARGH! OW!"

"Hurts, doesn't it Russell?"

"Yes Miss. A LOT Miss."

"Good. I'm very pleased to hear it. You're confirming that the punishment is proving effective."

"Oh it is, Miss. Very effective, Miss."

Russell's bum strained upwards even more and he parted his legs wider still, affording me an excellent view of his most private area of all, and an excellent opportunity to cane the more sensitive areas on each side of his wide crack. I knew from plenty of experience that if these soft parts were presented for the cane to punish, the results would be quite spectacular.

"I forgot to ask you to count the strokes, Russell. Perhaps you'd be good enough to do this for us in the time-honoured way. We'll start again."

Before he could reply, and without any warning, I whipped the supple cane right across the centre of

Russell's outstretched cheeks, producing a strangled gasp and a beautiful, clear red line marking the middle spot of both bum-cheeks.

THWHACK!

"AAAAAAAAAAAAAAAARGH! One Miss. Thank you, Miss."

As usual, I was delighted at how well the cane bit right into the submissively presented buttocks.

THWHACK!

"Two Miss," he uttered immediately, followed by "Thank you, Miss!"

Right away, the third stroke landed, just a tiny bit lower than the first two. Another thin line of pain burnt itself across Russell's bare bum, and his reaction confirmed the sting had increased and had quickly reached its peak – so far.

"AAAAAAAAAAAAAAAAAAARGH! Three Miss," he managed, with clear panic starting to show in his voice. He added mischievously, "Thank you Miss," and then gulped "I mean, thank you VERY much Miss".

His legs were now so far apart that I could clearly see his big balls hanging provocatively down, and I was able to notice the satisfying twitching in his cock as this third hard stroke found its target.

With no hesitation I whacked the cruel cane down again, whipping it with enthusiasm right in to Russell's soft cheeks, causing a real yell from the hapless recipient. This was a beautiful stroke, delivered perfectly horizontally, just as it should be, and again a little lower than before.

"AAAAAAAAAAAAAAAAAAAAARGH! OW! OUCH! OWWWWWWW!"

Russell's feet began to dance in the air and his exposed cheeks started to clench and unclench in a futile attempt to alleviate the burning fire that was consuming him. Oh how that cane stung!

"Oh, please Miss! I mean...thank you Miss!" Mike Russell's distress was clear for me to see and hear. I was really enjoying myself now, and the sight of those four vivid scarlet tramlines scorched across this handsome young man's hairy cheeks was starting to have an effect on me. I stared fixedly at the punished buttocks meekly presented, waiting for further torment.

I was tapping the cane now onto Russell's bum. My tapping began to turn into repetitive fast thwhacking as I said

"I'm waiting for the next number. You don't want me to go back and start again, do you?"

"Oh no Miss! Please not that Miss! Um... four Miss!"

Russell's statement of the next number was just in time.

"Good lad," I said quite warmly. "That was indeed stroke number four. I was beginning to wonder if you were losing count."

I followed this remark without a second's pause by a harder stroke, the hardest one yet. I aimed lower still this time and produced a very satisfying reaction. I was gradually working my way over the entire surface of both of Russell's gorgeous masculine bum-cheeks, lower down each time - and also slightly increasing the intensity of each stroke as well.

THWHACK!

"AAAAAAAAAAAARGH! OWWWWW! AAAAAAAH! Oh, please Miss. No Miss! Um ... I mean five MISS!" he shouted all at once.

I stroked the cane lightly up and down both of Mike Russell's cheeks and let the tip just start to enter his crack.

"Thank you Miss," he added just in time.

The two of us in the room knew this next was the final stroke, and Russell would surely have guessed that this stroke would be a memorable one. He was not disappointed.

"Bottom up a little higher still, please," I ordered.

Strangely, Russell needed no persuasion to do this. He was in fact already straining his arse as high as it would go, almost inviting the next stroke by offering his scalding cheeks in an even more provocative pose.

A few seconds elapsed during which time I chose my favourite spot to aim the final stroke of this superb six-of-the-best. I tapped the cane lightly across the crease where Russell's soft bum-cheeks met the tops of his thighs. Then ...

THWHACK!

The supple cane seemed to take on a life of its own as I whipped it along the very spot where Russell would be hoping to be able to sit down. This he would not now be doing for quite a while! Well-timed and perfectly accurate, the stroke was a beauty, although I say it myself.

Russell yelled, he kicked out, he gasped and squirmed while I looked on in satisfaction at my accuracy and skill.

"AAAAAAAAAAGH! OW! OW! OW! AAAAAAAAAAAAAGH!"

I was openly pleased with myself now as Russell's striped bum-cheeks frantically clenched and unclenched in front of me. Nothing he could do, however, alleviated the burning, scalding heat in his rear. His masculine, manly rump was now officially on fire!

"I'm waiting," was all I said.

"I'm very sorry Miss. Six Miss. Thank you Miss," came Russell's humbled reply. He was panting now, almost gasping for breath, but STILL sticking his flaming bum in the air.

"We'll have a breather now for a few minutes before we deal with your OTHER offences," I said calmly. "All this exertion is exhausting me."

Both of us remained still in a kind of stunned silence, while his hard, erect cock strained urgently upwards, dripping pre-cum.

"And you stay where you are," I told Russell firmly.

He whimpered in anticipation of what was still to come, but stayed completely still – except for his right hand which was now moving back and forth along the length of his thick, swollen member. This was something that I was NOT going to comment about. I knew Russell wouldn't actually cum. He wouldn't be stupid enough to do that, no matter how horny he felt. If he did so, the punishment that was still to come would have been absolutely intolerable. Even though I was adamant that he needed to be punished, I wanted him to benefit from the afternoon in as many ways as he could.

After a few minutes, I spoke again.

"Very well, Russell. As promised, we will now deal with your further misbehaviour."

"Yes Miss." His bottom stuck up further as he said this.

"There is the matter of your lewd language when you spoke to me just now about the disgusting graffiti you scrawled on the toilet wall."

"Yes Miss. I mean … yes please Miss. Please deal with that offence as well Miss."

"Oh I will, Russell. I'm going to deal with it VERY firmly. Don't you worry about that."

"Oh … thank you Miss. Thank you very much Miss."

"And finally there is the question of your impertinence when you first arrived this afternoon. I remember noticing a distinct grin on your face as we discussed you misbehaviour, and I remember saying that you would not be leaving with a grin by the time I had finished with you today. Do you remember me saying that, Russell?"

"Oh yes I do Miss. I DO remember Miss."

"Good. Then I'm sure you will also remember these next two strokes. Stick that bum of yours right up, Russell. Take hold of your cheeks and pull them apart for me. I'm going to apply these two additional strokes DOWN your crack."

"Oh No Miss. Please Miss."

"Do it, Russell."

The young man was whimpering quite loudly now, and the smirk had definitely left his face as he reached round and opened up his arse to the cruel attentions of my favourite cane. His hands gripped his beautiful buttocks and pulled them wide apart.

"Stay just like that, Russell. Keep your bum wide open until you've had BOTH of these strokes. If you let go of your cheeks after the first stroke, that stroke won't count and we'll start again."

Russell complied with every detail of my instruction and waited, clearly in some distress.

Thwhip!

The cruel cane did its excellent work, whipping DOWN the young man's open, hairy crack and with my experience and well-honed skill I was able to make the painful tip land right onto his exposed arse hole. It wasn't a hard stroke. It didn't need to be – and to have caned him hard in this sensitive area would have been dangerous and wrong. It was more of a thwip! than a real THWHACK! Just a deft flick of my wrist produced the result I wanted.

He squealed, gasped, writhed and wriggled – but still he remained defiantly in position, buttocks wide open, everything on show, beautifully displayed.

Thwip!

His second, slightly louder squeal told us both that the punishment was over.

"Well done, Russell," I said encouragingly. "You are forgiven completely. We've wiped the slate clean and you can get dressed."

Struggling to rise, shaking a little, and looking very submissive and compliant, the young man dressed in silence. There was no flicker of defiance on his face now. My cane could always be relied upon to produce a real change in behaviour. It was the most perfect instrument of punishment you could possibly desire.

When he was fully clothed, he came and stood in front of me.

"Good man, Russell," I said warmly. "You took that really well. Report to me at the same time tomorrow when I shall have a look at your marks. Hopefully, if they're still bright and clear, there will be no need for any more."

"Thank you Miss."

"And finally just the little matter of your imposition. As is always the tradition in this college, you will write a two thousand word essay in your very best handwriting and bring it with you when you report back tomorrow afternoon. The subject, as usual, is the effects and benefits of corporal punishment."

"Yes Miss. Thank you Miss."

"Good afternoon, Russell. And I would eat your supper standing up today, if I were you!"

The next story in this series is entitled "A Sore Bum for You, Stewart!" in which I describe in detail how I deal with a rather arrogant young man who needs bringing down a peg or two after he has been absent several times without permission and then told bare faced lies. He will certainly think twice before missing classes again after I have finished with him. He receives a highly embarrassing bare bottom spanking, and a hard and prolonged hairbrushing BEFORE a traditional six-of-the-best with my favourite whippy cane. Read all about it!

A Sore Bum for You, Stewart!

by Mistress Jade (with Mark Maguire)

One of the best perks available to me in my position as Senior Mistress at St Boniface's Sixth Form College is the pleasure of punishing the young men who so frequently misbehave during their time here.

Today I am dealing with Stewart Barlow, a slim, handsome young man with masculine good looks who is going to be punished for unauthorised absence and also for telling lies. This is a detailed account of the painful corporal punishment I gave him. He was foolish enough to miss several classes on account of his fondness for gambling. Instead of attending Miss Goddard's modern history lectures, for three weeks following, he spent the time in the local betting shop. When challenged, he told Miss Goddard that he had not left the premises but had been working in the library on each occasion. Thankfully, the CCTV evidence showed otherwise. He will shortly discover just how much my favourite cane burns and stings as it penetrates deep into his obediently presented, manly buttocks.

Our sixth formers are all over 18, and as young adults they benefit from the hard corporal punishments I administer regularly to their bare arses. All of them, with no exceptions, on reaching the age of eighteen, willingly signed our standard consent form agreeing to whatever physical discipline we, as tutors, see fit to administer. Even though they are grown men, rudeness, laziness, smoking, truancy, bad manners and many other offences still need dealing with on a frequent basis – and this I very much enjoy doing as a mature, dominant, sexy woman.

I punish each and every offence with painful corporal discipline which I always apply to bare bottoms – no exceptions. This aspect is often more of an ordeal for the young men to endure than the excruciating pain of one of my spankings or hard canings. They absolutely hate exposing their most private parts to an older woman.

Many of the young men have girlfriends who will always, sooner or later, hear all the details of a punishment their handsome boyfriend has suffered. Can you imagine how embarrassing that is! This is why I love my job so much – the feeling of complete power I have over my young charges, combined with the pure enjoyment of watching the distress of a young man as he meekly presents his bare bottom for me to punish as I see fit.

As Senior Mistress, I love using my favourite, thin, whippy cane and I adore causing red raw stripes to appear across their soft, firm male buttocks particularly if the buttocks I am punishing are beginning to be hairy. I enjoy producing angry raised weals that will make sitting down more or less impossible for quite a while after the apologetic and regretful young man has left my study, clutching his throbbing cheeks in a desperate but futile attempt to rub out the maddening, burning sting.

I take great pride in the accuracy of my canings and can almost always produce an equal effect on both cheeks. My hand spankings are never a soft option either. I persist with a spanking until I am sure I have got through to the recalcitrant young man over my knee. This only happens when he cries. It can take a long time for this to be achieved, but I always keep going until I do. "Spanked to tears" is my favourite motto and all the sixth formers in my charge know this.

Today I am dealing with Stewart Barlow, a young man who needs to learn a painful lesson. I will make sure he attends every one of Miss Goddard's lectures in future. The village betting shop will most definitely be out of bounds for him from now on! He will also think twice about telling lies when I have finished with him.

Here comes that nervous knock on my door. It's right on time. Stewart's appointment was for 4.00 pm and he knows the importance of punctuality.

"Enter!" I always utter just this one word when a young man is reporting for corporal punishment. It sets the tone for the whole encounter. "Come in" would be too informal.

"Ah Stewart. How nice to see you. To what do we owe the pleasure of this little meeting?"

"You told me to come at 4 o'clock, Miss."

"Come, Stewart? I hope you won't COME while you trousers and pants are down in my study. What you do when you return to your dormitory is your own affair of course."

"Yes Miss."

"You are here because of your several unauthorised absences."

"Yes Miss."

"And the bare faced lies you told Miss Goddard when she challenged you."

"Yes Miss."

"And you have been punished before for truancy, haven't you?"

Stewart looked dolefully down to the floor as he replied.

"Yes Miss. Only once, Miss."

"Are you suggesting that there is some merit in having been absent without permission only once?"

"No Miss."

"Then you are wasting my time by diverting this discussion unnecessarily."

"Yes Miss. Sorry Miss."

"You will be, Stewart."

"Yes I'm sure Miss."

"And how do you imaging we are going to deal with your truancy and your lies, Stewart? See if you can hazard a guess."

"Um ... not sure Miss."

"Oh but I think you ARE sure, Stewart, because you've been to see me at 4 o'clock before. You're wasting my time, young man. I will ask you again to tell us how you think I will deal with your disgraceful behaviour."

"Caning, Miss."

"Any particular KIND of caning, Stewart?"

"HARD, Miss. A good, HARD caning Miss!"

His eyes unmistakably lit up a little as he said this. Unperturbed, I issued a clear instruction.

"Drop your trousers and pants, put them neatly on that chair, and then come here."

"Yes Miss."

This was the first part of the session that I really enjoyed. Seeing a strong, handsome, masculine young man having to strip in front of me always started to turn me on. He quickly dropped his tight black trousers and stepped out of them. Placing them on the chair, I had the first glimpse of his beautiful buttocks as he slightly bent forward. He pulled his boxers down to reveal two magnificent arse globes, just slightly hairy but still mainly smooth. He was just 18 years old. A grown man who would shortly be reduced to tears as I built up a real raging heat in his bum.

He walked over and stood beside me.

"Over my knee, Stewart."

This took the handsome young man completely by surprise. He had mentally prepared himself for one of my excruciatingly painful canings. He hadn't expected the complete indignity of an over-the-knee spanking first.

"Oh Miss. Not a spanking, please Miss. I accept I'm going to be caned, Miss. Surely that's enough, Miss."

"Oh, you ACCEPT that, do you Stewart? How very kind of you. I will remind you that it's not for you to ACCEPT what punishment I decide to give. You will just take it, Stewart, no matter what you think. Do you understand?"

"Yes Miss. I do understand Miss."

His cock moved slightly as he said this. It had been sticking out just a little from under his shirt tail. Now it began to rise. Stewart, like many of my pupils, found my strict, humiliating dialogue horny and inexplicably arousing.

"We have two distinct misdeeds to punish today, and also two distinct roles in this encounter, Stewart. Your role is to present your bottom correctly and my role is to spank it – long and hard. Get over my knee Stewart and stick it up!"

He obeyed immediately, without further discussion. He wriggled a little into position so that his head was right down on the carpet and his gorgeous butt was presented perfectly right in the middle of my lap. I would smack now for a long time. I would smack him until he cried.

SMACK! SMACK! SMACK!

"This spanking will remind you not to miss your lessons, young man."

"Yes Miss."

"And I shouldn't need to tell you that Miss Goddard knows you are here in this humiliating position over an older woman's knee having your bare bottom smacked."

SMACK! SMACK! SMACK! SMACK!

I began to build up the rhythm and tempo, spanking every area of those two beautiful mounds of masculine flesh. He had a fine, handsome rump that was just crying out to be spanked – HARD.

"Remind us of my favourite motto please, Stewart." I said suddenly, stopping the spanking for a breather and lightly patting the hot cheeks instead.

"Spanked to tears, Miss!"

"Excellent, Stewart. Well remembered. And how near to tears are we at the moment, would you say?"

I felt his cock stiffen and press down fervently into my knees as I said this.

"Oh, not very near yet, Miss. I think we've got quite a long way to go."

"Good lad, Stewart," I said, with not a little amusement. "I think we understand each other very well."

"Oh yes Miss. Yes we do Miss."

"Good! Now young man, you won't be surprised to hear that my hand is getting quite sore with all this exertion."

"Not as sore as my bum, Miss."

"I shall ignore that remark, Stewart. However, the point is that I will need some assistance if we are to achieve the stated aim of this punishment. Get up, Stewart, and fetch the hairbrush."

"Oh Miss. Please no, Miss."

Both of us knew how extremely painful the hard wooden back of that hairbrush could be when applied vigorously to the bare, exposed buttocks of a naughty young man.

"Fetch it, Stewart."

He struggled to get off my lap, fell to the floor briefly, then picked himself up and walked over to the bookcase on the far wall. As he did so, his stiff cock bobbed invitingly up and down before him. It was clearly rock hard, and was already oozing just a little pre-cum. What would it be like once I had caned him?

He picked up the hairbrush that I kept on the top shelf in front of the encyclopaedias. Gingerly he walked back, handed it me politely, and then draped himself provocatively over my knees again.

"I'm going to give you something to think about when you consider visiting the village betting shop again during college hours. A burning bottom is what you need, young man, and I know of no better way of achieving that than a good, prolonged hairbrushing."

Blushing profusely, Stewart Barlow wriggled a little to get himself into the correct position that I always demanded for hairbrush spankings – head right down to the floor, arms out in front, and bottom pushed right UP and OUT for the painful attentions it was about to receive.

"Well done," I said encouragingly, lightly rubbing the flat, smooth surface of the hairbrush all over the soft, muscular cheeks I was about to smack HARD. "A little wriggling to get into position is entirely acceptable. However, I remind you young man that you are to keep still, once I really get going, no matter how much you want to avoid this little beauty and its excellent effects."

"Yes, Miss."

"As always, we need to agree upon why you are going to be punished in this painful and embarrassing way. Please confirm."

Stewart disliked this bit SO much, and I knew it. That was why I asked. He could only mumble agreement to what was about to happen and accept that it was a necessary prelude to his impending encounter with my whippy cane – all of which was taking place because of his unauthorised visits to the betting shop.

"I'm glad you agree with the necessity of this spanking, Stewart."

"Yes Miss. I do agree, Miss. I know it IS necessary, Miss."

"Good. Then we'll begin."

SMACK!

Without warning, the hard, unforgiving wooden brush landed right in the middle of Stewart' left cheek.

SMACK! SMACK!

Twice, in quick succession it visited the same spot on his right cheek.

Both cheeks were, of course, already very sore, red and inflamed from the prolonged hand spanking I'd just given them.

What's the perfect implement that delivers a searing, scorching spanking that'll make sitting down difficult for a long while afterwards? Why the hairbrush of course, and I am an expert in its use. One of the things that I always say makes the hairbrush so satisfying to use is the extreme pain and raging heat you can produce with the minimum of effort. Each smack produces an absolutely devastating effect with just a very swift and purposeful flick of the wrist.

SMACK, SMACK, SMACK!

"Do you remember when you were last over my knee?" I enquired nonchalantly as I smacked away, increasing both the speed and the severity all the time.

"Aaaaaah! Yes I do! Please Miss! No! AAAAAAAAARGH! OW! OUCH!"

SMACK, SMACK, SMACK, SMACK!

His cries were becoming increasingly urgent as both of his soft, masculine cheeks turned a deeper and deeper shade of red.

SMACK, SMACK, SMACK, SMACK, SMACK!

"PLEASE, Miss. I've learned my lesson I promise. AAAAAAAAARGH! No more, PLEEEEEASE!"

His desperate pleas fell on deaf ears as I merrily smacked away with more and more determination. As he struggled to cope, Stewart remembered my clear instruction NOT to wriggle. But how could he not? He summoned up all the strength that was within him to both cope with the maddening pain AND keep still – a near impossible task!

SMACK, SMACK, SMACK, SMACK, SMACK, SMACK!

Faster and harder smacks now. As the intensity built and built, I knew that Stewart knew what was coming next!

As always, I started directing the smacks DOWN onto the lowest part of his brightly burning cheeks. Soon the strokes were landing right on his crease – the spot where his buttocks met the tops of his manly legs. Stewart had big, slightly hairy thighs, which provided a sizeable area for me to work on with the back of that wonderful, terrible brush. Good, brisk, punitive strokes landed again and again on the same tender spots on the back of each of Stewart' manly thighs.

SMACK! SMACK! SMACK!

"Aaaaaaaaaaaaargh! Ow! Ouch! NO Miss! Please!"

My determined smacks were quicker still now, and even harder, resulting in gasps, yelps and desperate pleas from Stewart, who was bucking and bawling now across my knees.

"PLEEEEEEEASE, Miss! I'm sorry! I promise…. OW!"

I continued concentrating all the strokes really low down, hitting the same spots on each cheek over and over, faster and faster, reinforcing rather than spreading the pain.

He bucked and yelled, begging, crying, but all to no avail. Tears started to flow and I could see it was all he could do not to absolutely sob aloud.

"AAAAAAAAAAAAAAAARGH! Please! No more! PLEEEEEEEASE! I can't stand the hairbrush! You know that, Miss!"

"Yes I do. That's why I use it so regularly. Now keep that beautiful bottom of yours UP!"

SMACK, SMACK, SMACK!

Now the brush was busy on Stewart' beautiful bright-red bum cheeks again – and then on the backs of his thighs again– and that DID hurt! WOW! I certainly knew how to give a memorable hairbrushing, even though I say it myself.

As he gasped and yelled, pure horror came into Stewart' mind. He was soon going to have to present this sore bum of his to me, to have it caned.

Open sobbing poured out of him. "Oh stop, Miss. Please Miss. I've learnt my lesson Miss, really I have."

"Get up!" I suddenly commanded.

He struggled to his feet once again as I said ...

"My favourite motto, please Stewart. Say it again."

There was a long pause, while he regained something of his composure and wiped his eyes. Then he said softly

"Spanked to tears, Miss."

"Good man," I said quite warmly. "And we've certainly achieved our aim, haven't we?"

"Oh yes, definitely Miss!"

"I'm glad we agree. We'll have a break, I think. But the cane later for lying, don't forget, just to make sure you learn your lesson. No rubbing meanwhile."

As instructed, the young man in front of me made no attempt to rub his blazing bum. However, he rubbed his cock completely without shame.

It was clearly very hard but would have to stay that way until he had some privacy later. Right now, though, Stewart was taking advantage of the unwritten rule we had that allowed those who had taken their punishments well to gain some pleasure from the experience as well as the pain. The two of us in the room knew this and I gave him a full five minutes in which to relax – but not completely if you understand what I mean!

Eventually I said ...

"And now the cane."

Without any kind of protest, Stewart approached my big leather-topped table and stretched right across.

"Bottom up a little higher still, please," I ordered.

Strangely, Stewart needed no persuasion to do this. What a wonderfully well-disciplined young man he was becoming. He was in fact already straining his arse as high as it would go, almost inviting the caning by offering his scalding cheeks in an even more provocative pose. Was he actually taking pleasure from showing off his burning bruises and raw red cheeks?

"This is for lying, Stewart."

"Yes Miss."

A few seconds elapsed during which time I just admired the way his bum quivered, clenched and unclenched, meekly awaiting its painful fate. Then, when I was ready and not before, I chose my favourite spot to aim the strokes of this superb six-of-the-best.

I tapped the cane lightly across the crease where Stewart Barlow's soft bum-cheeks met the tops of his thighs. He immediately raised his throbbing arse even higher, offering more of his most sensitive part of all to the burning, smarting sting that he and I both knew he would soon be experiencing. Then ...

THWHACK!

The supple cane seemed to take on a life of its own as I whipped it along the very spot where Stewart and I both understood it would be most effective. The stroke was a beauty, although I say it myself.

Stewart yelled, he kicked out, he gasped and squirmed while I looked on in satisfaction at my accuracy and skill.

Again and again, five more times I whipped that superb cane HARD right across his sit-spot.

"AAAAAAAAAAGH! OW! OW! OW! AAAAAAAAAAAAAGH!"

I knew Stewart wouldn't actually cum. He wouldn't be stupid enough to do that, no matter how horny he felt. If he did so, the punishment would have been absolutely intolerable.

After a few minutes, I spoke again.

"Very well, Stewart. That completes your discipline for today."

"Yes Miss. Thank you very much, Miss."

"There is the matter of your return visit to me tomorrow."

"Yes Miss. I mean … yes please Miss. Please deal with me tomorrow as well Miss."

"You will return at the same time again tomorrow to present your bottom for inspection. If your marks are still nice and clear, we'll call it a day for now. However, if I feel they have faded too much, I shall apply the same punishments again. The hairbrushing AND the caning."

"Yes Miss. I know you'll deal with me very firmly, Miss."

"Oh I will, Stewart. I'm going to deal with you VERY firmly. Don't you worry about that."

"Oh ... thank you Miss. Thank you very much Miss. See you tomorrow Miss."

The next story in this series is entitled "Hold Out Your Hand, Neil!" in which I describe in detail how I deal with a cocky young man who needs a painful reminder to behave after he has been caught stealing from the village shop and being cheeky to our hard-working caretaker.. Neil will certainly think twice before doing that again after I have finished with him. Read all about it!

Hold Out Your Hand, Neil!

by Mistress Jade (with Mark Maguire)

One of the best perks available to me in my position as Senior Mistress at St Boniface Sixth Form College is the pleasure of punishing the young men who so frequently misbehave during their time here.

Today I am dealing with Neil Sheeran, a strapping lad with jet black hair and brown eyes who is going to discover the painful consequence of stealing. The young man's thieving was mercifully witnessed by our catering supervisor, Mrs Stockley who I shall invite to witness Neil's punishment.

Our sixth formers are all over 18, and as young adults they benefit from the hard corporal punishments I administer regularly to their bare bottoms. All of them, with no exceptions, on reaching the age of eighteen, willingly signed our standard consent form agreeing to whatever physical discipline we, as tutors, see fit to administer. Even though they are grown men, rudeness, laziness, smoking, truancy, bad manners and many other offences still need dealing with on a frequent basis – and this I very much enjoy doing as a mature, dominant, older woman who's always very much in charge.

I deal with each and every offence with painful corporal punishment. If I decide to punish the young man's bottom, I always insist that the bottom is bare – no exceptions. This aspect is often more of an ordeal for the young men to endure than the excruciating pain of one of my spankings or hard canings. Sometime, however, I decide a hand caning is called for. This can be the best punishment to give in certain circumstances. Today is one of those occasions.

Many of the young men have girlfriends who will always, sooner or later, hear all the details of a punishment their handsome boyfriend has suffered. Can you imagine how embarrassing that is! This is why I love my job so much – the feeling of complete power I have over my young charges, combined with the pure enjoyment of watching the distress of a young man as he meekly presents his bare bottom or his outstretched hands for an older woman to punish as I see fit.

I love using my favourite, thin, whippy cane and I adore causing red raw stripes to appear across their palms or their soft, firm male buttocks particularly if the buttocks I am punishing are beginning to be hairy. I enjoy producing angry raised weals that will make sitting down more or less impossible for quite a while after the apologetic and regretful young man has left my study, clutching his throbbing cheeks in a desperate but futile attempt to rub out the maddening, burning sting.

I take great pride in the accuracy of my canings and can almost always produce an equal effect on both cheeks or both hands. I also use a favourite three-tailed tawse to punish hands when I fancy a change. My spankings are never a soft option either. I persist with a spanking until I am sure I have got through to the recalcitrant young man over my knee. This only happens when he cries. It can take a long time for this to be achieved, but I always keep going until I do. "Spanked to tears" is my favourite motto and all the sixth formers in my charge know this.

Here then is my detailed account of how I dealt with Neil Sheeran, our insolent young man who thinks it's ok to steal from a shop and then be rude to someone who works hard over long hours for little reward. Our catering supervisor, Mrs Stockley was in the shop at the time of the theft and, unknown to young Neil, saw him slip several items into his pocket.

It's 11.00 am and there's a rather tentative knock at my door. I go over to a large plant pot in the corner of the room and withdraw my favourite senior cane. Thirty inches long, with a traditional crooked handle, it packs an excruciating sting with every fiercely applied stroke. I place it on my desk where Neil will see it as soon as he walks in. This always sets the tone of the meeting!

"Ah, Neil. How good to see you. Come in, won't you?"

There is no reply to my opening remark. The obviously nervous young man walks in to my study, all the time avoiding my gaze.

"Stand there, Neil. Hands by your sides, shoulders back, head up straight. Perhaps you will begin by telling me why you are here."

"You sent for me, Miss. You told me yesterday that I was to report at this time this morning."

"Indeed I did, Neil, and the fact that your appointment with me was made a day in advance should have given you a clue as to what was going to happen to you while you were here."

"Yes Miss."

"What do you see on my desk, Neil?"

"Some books, two pens, a blotter and a little dust, Miss." He grinned very slightly as he said this, but still averted his gaze.

"How dare you, Neil! How dare you try to play verbal games with me! You are here for stealing, and to rudeness to Mrs Stockley, and now you have been openly insolent to me. What ELSE do you see?"

"A senior cane, Miss."

"Exactly, Neil. And why do you suppose it is there?"

"To punish me, Miss."

"Correct, Neil. To punish you severely. And which part of you, do you suppose, is going to experience that severe punishment?"

"My bum, Miss – er I mean bottom Miss."

"And is there any particular adjective that will apply to your bottom this morning, Neil?"

"Attractive, Miss – but that doesn't just apply this morning!"

This time Neil looked me straight in the face as he said this, with a not at all unfriendly smile. He and I had grown to understand each other very well indeed over a number of corporal punishment sessions he had attended.

"Mmmmmmmmm," I replied with just a little amusement. "I'll be the judge of that, young man," I added.

"I know you will, Miss. And before you go to the trouble of asking me a second time what adjective will apply to my butt, I can tell you right away. Bare, Miss – and sore Miss, I expect."

"Oh you can certainly expect your bottom to be sore, Neil. You can more than expect that, you can be absolutely sure. I am going to make your bottom so sore this morning that you won't want to sit down for the rest of the week. And if you do ever try to sit down any time in the next few days, your unbelievably sore bottom will serve as a wonderful reminder to you not to steal and to always be polite to your superiors."

"Yes Miss."

"We are expecting Mrs Stockley to join us any time around now, but before she arrives, let me just explain that it is not just your bottom that will be sore when you leave this room in half an hour's time."

"What do you mean, Miss?" For the first time, the self-assured young man looked concerned.

"Your rudeness to Mrs Stockley will result in a good dose of the senior cane, Neil. You will undoubtedly have been expecting that."

"Oh I have been, Miss. I've been thinking about little else since you gave me my appointment yesterday. A good dose of your cane was on my mind all through the night, Miss."

"I'm pleased to hear it, Neil. However, we also have to deal with your stealing and also your downright insolence to me this morning."

"I was just having a bit of a laugh, Miss."

"You are entitled to laugh at times that are appropriate to do so, Neil. However, while you are being told off by your Senior Mistress is definitely NOT one of those times. For stealing, I am going to punish your thieving hands, Neil, and for your downright insolence to me just now I will add an additional punishment that you are not going to like at all."

The young man's face went white.

"You're not going to cane my hands, are you Miss?"

Real panic was now written all over his handsome young face. I was pleased to be getting through to him at last. The trouble with Neil was that he had become a real aficionado of the cane. I knew he adored its intensely painful and penetrating sting across his sturdy masculine buttocks, and this had had a stimulating effect on his cock the last three times he'd reported to me to be punished. Both of us were happy to accept this situation. It was not an uncommon response in a horny young man.

The problem was, though, that this developing fetish of his meant it was difficult to punish him properly for the offences he kept committing. I didn't mind the mainly good-hearted banter he'd had with me, but I couldn't have our students thinking they could be rude to our catering supervisor without dire consequences.

"I shall cane your hands if I think it's appropriate, Neil. That's my right as Senior Mistress."

"Yes Miss, I know it is Miss. I know hand caning is in the college discipline guidebook Miss, but that's going to be just too painful to be fair, Miss."

"I shall decide what's fair, Neil."

I could see his mind racing to think of a reasonable objection that might save him from this impending agony.

"Don't you think hand caning is dangerous, Miss?"

"Dangerous? For whom?"

"Me, Miss. I mean, you might strike my fingers Miss. You could do real damage."

"My cane never damages your bottom, Neil. It causes unbelievable pain, I know, and produces some really beautiful stripes – but that's all par for the course, so to speak. It never causes any real damage or lasting ill-effects. Wouldn't you agree, Neil?"

"Oh, yes Miss. What you say is absolutely right, Miss."

"Good. As a frequent recipient, I'm so glad you agree."

At this, I picked up the cane which had been lying in readiness to be put into service. I bent it into a perfect arc and let it spring back again. Then with a menacing "swoosh" I swished it through the air.

"I think this would hurt hands quite a lot more than it hurts bottoms," I said casually.

"Oh ... please Miss. I promise I'll be good, Miss. Really I will, Miss. I'll never steal again, Miss and I'll never be rude to Mrs Stockley again — or you, Miss. Only PLEASE don't cane my hands, I beg you, Miss."

I was really pleased to have reduced this usually quite cocky young man to such a state of total submission.

Just then, there was another knock at my door. A confident one this time, in complete contrast to the rather timid knock of this young man who had turned up to be punished.

I walked over to the door and opened it.

"Mrs Stockley. Do come in. Thank you for joining us."

The catering supervisor was a burly woman, well into middle age. Heavily built, she had the typical, rather swarthy complexion of a woman who spends a lot of time outdoors. Her grey hair was tied into a bun on the top, and her face was the face of a woman who had lived.

"We were just discussing hand caning, Mrs Stockley. Can you help us with any facts about this particular practice?"

Mrs Stockley grinned from ear to ear. She looked over at the arrogant young man who had treated her with not a little contempt on several occasions. How sweet it was now, to see him squirming with embarrassment as we casually discussed something that would cause him such absolute agony and distress.

"It was very common for the young men when I was at agricultural college," Mrs Stockley confirmed. "I met my husband to be there, as you know, and he only had it once and, bloody hell, it hurt like the very devil, he said. He'd been really cheeky as a student. I guess he thought as he was officially a young man that he could get away with it. He was 18, you see, when I'm sorry to say, he was downright insolent to one of the tutors. He didn't think they still caned you when you were 18, but of course they did. And most of the canings at our particular college were carried out on the hands. Boy did it hurt him! You can be sure he was NEVER rude again after that."

"Well, thank you Mrs Stockley. You've been very helpful," I replied. "You've confirmed what I think we all knew already – and that is that a good caning on the outstretched hands always produces results. Always changes behaviour for the better."

The catering supervisor and I grinned at each other. Then we both looked at the recalcitrant young man in front of us.

"Please Miss," he said. "I'll take any other punishment you'll give Miss. Only please don't cane my hands. You're really frightening me, Miss. I just don't think I could stand it, Miss."

"Young men HAD to stand it years ago. There was no choice. No question. It was a very standard punishment." Mrs Stockley spoke this time.

"And this particular young man's hands are THIEVING hands, as you told me yourself Mrs Stockley," I added. "How lucky it was that you witnessed Neil pocketing those packets of salted peanuts."

We all stood in silence for a while. I could almost hear young Neil's heart beating as rapidly as it undoubtedly was. Finally I said ...

"I think we've kidded you along for long enough, Neil. I'm NOT going to cane your hands."

"Oh thank you Miss. Thank you so much Miss." The young man almost wept with relief.

"Hand caning was indeed a very frequent punishment in the old days, Neil, but in those times no concern was shown for the damage it could often do. As you said just now, the cane could easily strike the outstretched fingers and could therefore even break bones if the strokes were hard. A foolish and irresponsible practice, if you ask me. In my opinion, the bare, well-presented buttocks of a sturdy young man are just made for hard caning. Young men's bare bums are just crying out to be caned, don't you think Neil?"

"Oh I do Miss. I agree completely Miss. Thank you Miss. Can I bend over for you now, Miss?"

Neil's confidence had returned, along with his irresistible, cheeky smile.

"All in good time, Neil. I said I'm not going to cane your hands, and I will keep my word - but I AM going to punish them. I'm going to tawse them, Neil, and Mrs Stockley is going to watch."

"Oh Miss!"

"MORE objections, Neil? I would make up your

mind to be completely compliant from now on, if I were you. You said you didn't want your hands caned, but that's as far as it goes. You're getting the tawse – right now."

"I don't even know what a tawse is, Miss."

"Well you'll soon find out. My favourite three-tailed tawse is in the top drawer over there. Bring it to me please."

The nervous young man walked over to the cupboard and opened the top drawer. He carefully withdrew a well-worn Scottish leather tawse about 18 inches long. The business part was cut into three tails of about 12 inches, leaving a convenient handle part for the disciplinarian to hold while administering painful punishments.

"The beauty of the tawse is that it's the edges of the tails that inflict the most pain. That's why I like a three-tailed rather than a two-tailed. More edges. More pain. Come over here, Mrs Stockley where you can see the effects from close quarters. Stand just to the side so that you're out of the firing line, so to speak. I flick it back right over my shoulder. Now for a practical demonstration. Hold out your hand, Neil."

There was a very long pause while the terrified young man wrestled with himself. Could he make himself submit in this humiliating way? Finally he spoke.

"Which hand Miss?"

"It doesn't matter, Neil. You're getting it on both. Hold out one of your hands, palm outstretched upwards. If you ever do this, Mrs Stockley, tell the young man to stretch his fingers down a little, which brings the palm of his hand UP. Then bring the tawse down smartly right across the middle of his outstretched palm. If you do this right, this will cause him to yelp – like this."

Thwhack!

"Ow!"

"Now hold out your other hand so that I can punish that one as well in the same way."

Neil gingerly complied.

Thwhack!

"As you can guess, Mrs Stockley, both his hands will now be burning.
I can tell you it's very difficult to hold out your hand a second time when it is already smarting so much – isn't it, Neil!"

"Yes Miss."

"But you're going to do just that, Neil. Hold the first hand out again."

Thwhack!

Each time I brought the tawse down smartly along the length of his fingers so that the cruel tips of the tails landed right into his palm.

"Ow! Ouch! Oh Miss!"

"Now the OTHER hand again, Neil."

Thwhack!

"Aaaaaaaaaah! Oh please Miss!"

"His rather vocal response tells us that my tawse is getting through to him, wouldn't you say Mrs Stockley?"

"Yes, definitely. A very rude young man is now starting to learn his lesson."

"Yes, just STARTING. We've got a long way to go yet, before he's learnt it completely. Obviously, I tawse each hand in turn each time, so that alternate hands feel the pain and heat. One stroke on the left. One stroke on the right. Then a second stroke on the left. Then a second stroke on the right. etc. etc. So ... Neil, the first hand again if you would be so kind."

I was so much into this scenario now, that I put an extra effort into these final two strokes, really smacking the cruel tawse viciously down along the whole length of each of his burning hands.

Thwhack!

"Aaaaaaaaaaaaah! Ow! Oooooooooo!"

"And now the other hand for its final treatment, please."

The young man's hand was visibly trembling and shaking as he ever so gingerly held it out yet again. The fingers and the whole surface of his soft palm were glowing bright red.

Thwhack!

"AAAAAAAAAAAAAAAAAAAAARGH!"

"Does the hand tawsing have the desired curative effect, Neil or are you still planning even more bad behaviour?" I enquired.

"Oh no Miss. Never again Miss. I'll never be rude again Miss. My hands hurt too much for that, Miss."

"Good. If there is further disobedience, I may decide to give corner time or award a couple of hundred lines. These can be very difficult to write when you've just had the palms of your hands tawsed. For example, 'I must show complete obedience to my tutors, and I must show complete respect to our catering supervisor'. Try writing that 200 times with your hands throbbing, Neil! If you displease me enough to earn a hand tawsing, you'll be very sorry if you also earn yourself 200 lines as well."

"Oh I won't Miss. I'll be completely obedient to you Miss. I'll do whatever you say, Miss. Only please don't tawse my hands any more, Miss. It BURNS Miss. My hands are so hot and sore, Miss!"

"I know, Neil. That's the whole idea. That's how we teach you manners in this college. Remember that, won't you, Neil."

"Oh I will, Miss."

"Good. Now to your well-deserved caning for this morning, young man. You may like to come over here, Mrs Stockley, to see this different technique from close range."

The catering supervisor walked over nearer to where I was positioned, waiting, with my favourite cane in my hand. Meanwhile, without being asked, Neil dropped his trousers and pants, stepped out of them and then positioned himself over my desk, stretched right across, up on tiptoe, arse in the air. He parted his legs wide and pushed his bum up and out, absolutely inviting the attentions of my thin, whippy cane.

"Now Neil, I'm going to give you six strokes, and they will all be hard ones. They will be applied rapidly, in quick succession, without any time in between to recover or to prepare yourself for the next. I've perfected this technique now, after lots of practice, and I know how to deliver each stroke just at the moment when the previous one has blossomed into its most intensely painful effect."

"Yes Miss."

"I will also apply all six strokes very low down, right across your crease, just where your bottom meets the top of your legs. You'll feel these, Neil."

"Yes Miss. Thank you, Miss."

Very lightly I placed the thin, flexible cane just where it was going to land. Neil flinched and clenched his buttocks which were trembling in fearful anticipation.

"Don't clench! Relax your bum!" I snapped impatiently.

Mrs Stockley walked over to stand beside me, to gain an excellent vantage point.

Then, suddenly …

THWHACK!

THWHIPP!

THWHACK!

THWHIPP!

THWHACK!   ... and finally ...

THWHACK!

Neil let out a blood curdling yell.

"AAAAAAAAAARGH! Ow! Ow! Ouch! Aaaaaaah! Oh Miss! It hurts Miss! It hurts SO much Miss! I'm sorry Miss! I won't be rude again EVER Miss. I promise. Only don't cane me any more Miss. PLEASE Miss!"

I looked over at Mrs Stockley and we both smiled as I said

"I think we've achieved the desired result!"

I ran my fingers along the length of the thin supple cane that had achieved the result I'd referred to and placed it gently on the table where it waited in readiness for its next application to the meekly displayed buttocks of a regretful young man.

The cane's work done for now, it lay there peacefully until the next time it would be needed to inflict intense fiery pain with its harsh caress.

"You may stand up," I said to the whimpering young man "and rub your bum as much as you like."

Neil rose gingerly and clutched his scorched, throbbing buttocks in a futile attempt to assuage the ferocious burning fire within them. It was hard for him to know which part of him was hotter – his hands or his arse.

"And now we come to your insolence to me when you first arrived this morning," I announced.

The humiliated and subdued young man stood before me, his semi-tumescent cock starting to poke through the front of his shirt.

"Are your hands still sore and stinging, Neil?" I asked casually.

"Yes Miss. A lot Miss. And my bum Miss."

"Well young man, you can use one of those sore, stinging hands to write for me two hundred times 'I must not be rude to my Senior Mistress when she is about to discipline me'."

"Oh Miss!"

"Bring the imposition to me at 10 o'clock tomorrow morning, at which time I shall take a look at your arse. If the stripes from my expert caning are not still clear, I shall give you another six strokes – harder."

"Yes Miss. Thank you Miss."

"Pull up your pants and trousers and make yourself decent again," I instructed. "Well done, Neil. I think you've learnt your lesson."

"Oh I have Miss. Definitely Miss. And thank you Miss. Thank you VERY much for disciplining me Miss. You're a WONDERFUL disciplinarian, Miss!"

"I know."

THE END

Mistress Jade and Mark Maguire have written numerous books on their favourite subject – adult discipline and corporal punishment. Enjoy them all at www.markmaguirebooks.co.uk

Printed in Great Britain
by Amazon

49305554R00056